When Eric's Mom Fought Cancer

STORY AND PICTURES BY

JUDITH VIGNA

ALBERT WHITMAN & COMPANY, MORTON GROVE, ILLINOIS

With love and thanks to Enid Zuckerman.

OTHER BOOKS BY JUDITH VIGNA

Black Like Kyra, White Like Me

Boot Weather

Grandma Without Me

I Wish Daddy Didn't Drink So Much

Mommy and Me by Ourselves Again

My Big Sister Takes Drugs

Nobody Wants a Nuclear War

Saying Goodbye to Daddy

She's Not My Real Mother

Designed by Lucy Smith.

Text and illustrations © 1993 by Judith Vigna.
Published in 1993 by Albert Whitman & Company,
6340 Oakton Street, Morton Grove, Illinois 60053-2723.
Printed in the United States of America.
10 9 8 7 6 5 4 3 2 1

Library of Congress Cataloging-in-Publication Data

Vigna, Judith.
    When Eric's mom fought cancer / Judith Vigna.
       p.   cm.
    Summary: A ski trip with his father helps a young boy who feels
angry and afraid when his mother gets sick with breast cancer.
       ISBN 0-8075-8883-0
       [1. Cancer—Fiction.   2. Parent and child—Fiction.] I. Title.
    PZ7.V67Wh   1993
    [E]—dc20   Ages 4 - 8
                                        93-6533
                                          CIP
                                          AC

A Note for Grownups

While advances are being made in the diagnosis and treatment of breast cancer, the disease can nonetheless be devastating for the whole family.

When the person who has cancer is the mother or caretaker of a young child, there's the added stress of trying to ease the youngster's fears at a time when the patient herself needs comfort and reassurance. And when other family members become overwhelmed, children can feel even more confused and rejected and see their lives as upended. In addition to imagining the loss of their mother, they might blame themselves for the illness or fear "catching" it.

Recognizing these concerns, many medical centers and agencies offer support services for patients living with cancer. Parents can learn how to talk realistically and hopefully with their children. Letting them express feelings of guilt, sadness, and anger; assuring them they'll be loved and cared for, no matter what; suggesting tasks that make them feel involved and needed; encouraging them to do things they enjoy—these are some of the ways families facing cancer can help young children to help themselves.

More information can be obtained from The American Cancer Society, 19 West 56th Street, New York, N.Y. 10019 (212-586-8700); The National Cancer Institute, Building 31, Room 10A24, Bethesda, Maryland (1-800-4-CANCER); Cancer Care, Inc., 1180 Avenue of the Americas, New York, N.Y. 10036 (212-221-3300).

Eric watches fat, wet flakes of snow fall outside his window.

His father had promised him skiing lessons. But winter's almost over, and Eric's never used the new skis he got for his birthday.

That's because his mother's gone to the hospital again.

Back in the fall, a sad thing happened. Eric's mother had to have an operation.

"Mommy has a disease called cancer," Daddy told him. "The doctors must cut away a bad tumor in her breast to help her get well."

Eric was very, very scared. "Are you going to die, Mommy?" he asked her.

His mother was still for a moment, then she said, "My doctor expects that I'll be fine. Nobody wants to get cancer, and some people do die. But lots of women who are sick like me live for a long time, as long as anyone."

"I don't want you to go to the hospital," Eric said. He started to cry.

Then his parents cried a little, too, and they all held each other.

The morning of his mother's operation,
Grandma came to stay with Eric. His stomach felt
wobbly, and he couldn't eat the waffles Grandma
made.

"What time is it?" he asked her over and over.

At last, at two o'clock, his father called from
the hospital. Mommy was all right, he said, and in
a few days Eric could visit her.

Eric couldn't wait.

The hospital was big and quiet. Eric was
allowed to stay just a few minutes, but there was
time to give his mother some water and tell her
about the neighbor's new puppy.

She hugged him gently because the place
where the doctor had cut was still sore.

"I've missed you so much!" she said.

After almost a week, Eric's mother came home. But sometimes she didn't feel like playing with him, and she had to lie down a lot.

To cheer her up, Eric made a funny drawing of a ski racer. "Come and help me put it on the refrigerator!" he said to his mom.

"Not right now," she said. "Can't you see I'm trying to rest?"

Grandma heard them talking, and she called Eric into the kitchen. "Mommy loves you, but she's tired and sad," she told him. "We'll have to try to be patient until she's herself again."

Sometimes Eric thought that time would never come. And just when his mother did begin to feel better, she had to start going back to the hospital for treatments to help stop new bad tumors from growing.

That was weeks ago, and now she's *still* getting treatments. She doesn't have to stay overnight at the hospital, but when she comes home she is more tired than ever. Sometimes she is sick to her stomach, and even more scary, some of her hair has fallen out. She wears a turban so no one can see how her scalp looks.

Today Eric feels sad and lonely, even though Grandma has come to stay with him while his parents go to the hospital.

He watches them climb into the car. "How much longer will Mommy have to get her treatments?" he asks.

"We don't know exactly, but probably through the summer," Grandma says. "The doctors are trying to fight that mean old cancer every way they can."

Soon there's a soft white blanket of snow on the lawn. Will he ever get to try his new skis? Eric wonders.

By three o'clock there is enough snow to build
a snowman in the backyard.

Eric rolls it into three snowballs, two giant ones
and a smaller one for the head. Grandma finds
one of his mother's turbans to use as a hat, and
Eric adds a twig nose and ski pole arms.

He wants to surprise his mother when she gets
home.

It is getting dark when his parents drive up. Eric meets them at the front door. "Come and see what I made!"

"Tomorrow," his mother says, kissing him. "I have to lie down now."

"You always have to lie down!" Eric yells. He runs outside and grabs a ski pole. "It's a lousy snowman, anyway!" He swings, and the snowman's head crashes to the ground.

Eric starts to cry just as Grandma comes outside.

"I'm sorry I got mad," he tells her.

Grandma hugs him. "It's okay," she says. "Mommy understands. She would have come to look at your snowman, but she's sick to her stomach right now. She'll feel better soon."

Eric knows this, but it's so hard to wait.

The next morning, Eric sees his father carrying skis to the car.

"Want to come to the mountains with me?" Daddy asks.

Eric wants to ski more than almost anything, but he worries. "Won't Mommy be lonely all by herself?"

"Grandma will be here, and Mom's friend from work is coming to visit." His father grins. "The trip is Mommy's idea. She says we need time out, both of us."

When they get to the mountains, Eric would
like to go to the top of the slope right away. But
first he must learn to make a wedge with his skis
so he can stop anywhere. And he must practice
making turns.

It's hard! There are many bumps, many
tumbles. But he watches his father and does as he
says. After lunch they are ready to ski from the top.

The chairlift is a bit scary, but it is slower than
a merry-go-round, and his father holds him firmly.

Eric feels like an astronaut floating above the trail.

He slides off the lift without falling, and he starts down the hill. His skis are wings on his feet.

"Watch me, Daddy!" he shouts.

When he looks back, he skids and plops into the snow. But even that is fun, now that he has learned how to fall down and get up by himself.

It's getting cold, so they go to the lodge for hot chocolate.

Eric spots a girl with a hat shaped like a bear's head. He remembers a time before his mother's operation. He had pretended to be a bear and had squeezed his mother's chest until she had laughed and said, "Stop—you're killing me!"

"One time I squeezed Mom too hard," he tells his father. "Did I make her get sick?"

"No, Eric. Bumps and bruises don't cause cancer. Nothing you did made Mommy ill."

"Can I catch cancer from her?"

"No way." His dad ruffles Eric's hair. "Cancer isn't catching, like chickenpox or a cold."

In the gift shop, Eric sees another special hat.
It has two woolen pigtails—a hat with hair!

He wants to buy it for his mother, but he has
only a dollar. His father gives him what he needs.

"You've picked just the right present," he tells
Eric.

The hat fits his mother perfectly.

"It's great!" she says. "I'll wear it until my hair grows back. But maybe that won't be too long—the doctor says my treatments are going well. So then I'll use it for a ski hat."

"When?" Eric asks.

"Next winter, I hope." His mother smiles. "When I go to the mountains with Daddy and you."

It is getting dark when his parents drive up. Eric meets them at the front door. "Come and see what I made!"

"Tomorrow," his mother says, kissing him. "I have to lie down now."

"You always have to lie down!" Eric yells. He runs outside and grabs a ski pole. "It's a lousy snowman, anyway!" He swings, and the snowman's head crashes to the ground.

Eric starts to cry just as Grandma comes outside.

"I'm sorry I got mad," he tells her.

Grandma hugs him. "It's okay," she says. "Mommy understands. She would have come to look at your snowman, but she's sick to her stomach right now. She'll feel better soon."

Eric knows this, but it's so hard to wait.